The Biggest Nose

Story and Pictures by

KATHY CAPLE

HOUGHTON MIFFLIN COMPANY

BOSTON   1985

To my mother and father,
my sister Margaret,
and brothers, John and Jim

Library of Congress Cataloging in Publication Data

Caple, Kathy.
 The biggest nose.

 Summary: Eleanor the elephant is self-conscious about
her large nose after she is teased by Betty the hippo-
potamus, but she overcomes her sensitivity when she
realizes Betty has the biggest mouth.
 1. Children's stories, American. [1. Nose — Fiction.
2. Elephants — Fiction. 3. Animals — Fiction] 1. Title.
PZ7.C17368Bi 1985 [E] 84-19745
ISBN 0-395-36894-4

"One, two, three, four, five," counted Eleanor
softly to herself. She was holding her breath and
trying to keep from sneezing. It was reading period
and everyone was supposed to be quiet.

"Six, seven, eight, nine," continued Eleanor,
and just as she was about to say ten, she sneezed.
Everyone burst out laughing.

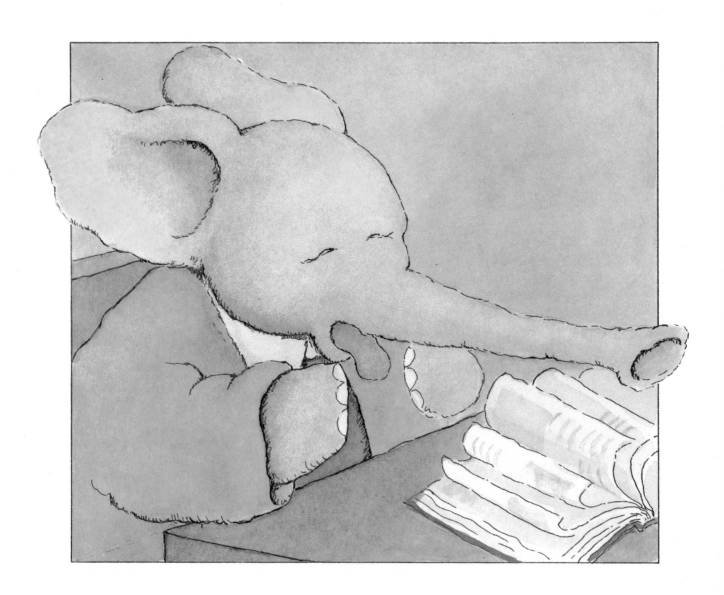

"It sounds like the school band tuning up," said Harold.

"And Eleanor is the trumpet," added Lizard.

"Doesn't her nose look just like a trumpet?"

"No," said Betty. "Her nose is too big to be a trumpet.
It's more like a tuba.
In fact, Eleanor has the biggest nose in the whole school."

"I do not!" said Eleanor.
"Oh, yeah?" said Betty.
"Name someone whose nose is bigger."
Eleanor thought for a minute.
"I know! My sister, Hilda.

She's an elephant, too, and she's in the next
grade so I'm sure her nose is bigger."
"How do you know?" asked Betty.
"Have you ever measured it?"
"Well, no," said Eleanor, "but —"

"You'd better know by tomorrow morning," said Betty,
"because we're going to do some measuring ourselves,
and if you're wrong, you'll be sorry."
Eleanor was worried.

That afternoon when Eleanor got home from school,
she went straight up to Hilda's room.
"Hilda!" she said, "get a ruler and hurry."
"What for?" said Hilda.
"I want to measure your nose," Eleanor said.
"Are you crazy?" said Hilda.

But she let Eleanor measure her nose.
"Twelve inches plus nine inches. That equals twenty-one inches," said Eleanor. "Now you measure mine."

Hilda measured Eleanor's nose. "Let's see...
It's exactly twenty-three inches."
"Are you sure?" asked Eleanor.
Hilda measured again. "Yes. It's twenty-three inches."
It was true. Eleanor's nose was bigger than
Hilda's. It must be the biggest nose in
the whole school.

"It's not so terrible," said Hilda. "Your
nose is probably just growing faster than the
rest of you. I wouldn't worry about it. Now
leave me alone. I have homework to do."
"That's no help at all," said Eleanor. She ran to the
bathroom and locked the door behind her.

"Dumb old elephant nose! I'll make this nose look smaller if it's the last thing I do."

And she took her nose and turned it up and down, and over and under, and every way possible.

Then she tied her nose in a knot.

It was shorter, but it looked very silly.

"I was better off before," said Eleanor.

She tried to undo the knot, only it wouldn't come out.

"Oh, dear!" thought Eleanor, "I can't let anybody see me like this. Please, knot, please come out."

Just then, her sister knocked on the door.
"Come on, Eleanor, let me in. You've been in
the bathroom long enough. There are other
animals around here!"
Eleanor did not know what to do.

She grabbed a towel and threw it over her
head and nose. She opened the door.
"It's about time," said Hilda.
"I was washing my head," said Eleanor.
"You were, were you? And that's my towel you
were using!"

Hilda pulled it away from Eleanor.
Then she saw her nose.
"Eeek!" said Hilda. "Look what you've done!
You're so weird."

"Mamma, Mamma," Hilda cried, running down the stairs.
"Eleanor has her nose all tied in a knot and it looks
really awful!"

"What?" said her mother, and she ran up the stairs
behind Hilda.

"My baby!" screamed Eleanor's mother.

"What's all the commotion?" her father wanted to know.

Then he saw Eleanor.

"We've got to do something," he cried.
You hold her feet and I'll grab the knot.
Now one, two, three, pull!"

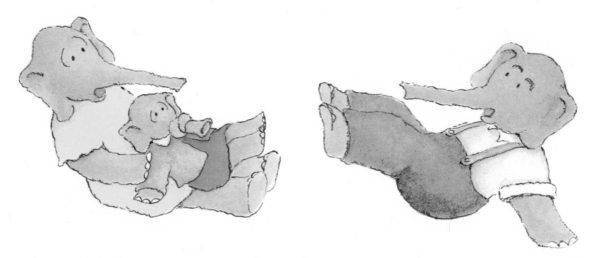

But it was no use. If anything, the knot was tighter.

"It's much too swollen," said her mother.
"We need some ice to make it smaller."

And they ran to the kitchen for some ice.
"Ohhh, that's cold," said Eleanor.
Soon all the ice had melted and still
her nose was in a knot.

"We need to make it more slippery," said her father.

"Let's try peanut oil."

He poured the oil all around the knot.

Eleanor wiggled her nose,

but they still couldn't get the knot untied.

"We may never get it out," said Hilda.
"She'll be this way for the rest of her life."
Suddenly Eleanor's nose began to tickle.
She started to sneeze.

"AAAAHHHHCHOOOOOEY!"
The knot came out.